Distant Feathers

Written and Illustrated by Tim Egan

Enjoy!

Tim Egan

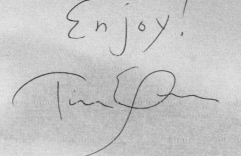

Houghton Mifflin Company
Boston 1998

For Tom, Mariellen, Peter, Jeanine, David, JoAnn, & Doug
—T. E.

The text of this book is set in 16 point Janson.
The illustrations are ink and watercolor on paper.

Library of Congress Cataloging-in-Publication Data
Egan, Tim.
Distant feathers / written and illustrated by Tim Egan.
p. cm.
Summary: Sedrick is visited by an enormous, annoying bird that
wreaks havoc on the town, but when the bird is presumed dead after a
violent hurricane, Sedrick finds that he misses it.
ISBN 0-395-85808-9
[1. Birds—Fiction. 2. Humorous stories.] I. Title.
PZ7.E2815Di 1998
[E]—DC21 97–8517 CIP AC

Manufactured in the United States of America
HOR 10 9 8 7 6 5 4 3 2 1

One Tuesday evening about seven years ago, Sedrick Van Pelt was quietly writing in his journal while trying to ignore the tapping sound on his window. It was a rather windy night, and he assumed it was just a tree hitting the house.

But it wasn't a tree.

When he turned to see what was causing the tapping, his mouth dropped open and he screamed.

Staring into his window was the face of the largest bird anyone had ever seen—a bird twice the size of a house, maybe larger, depending on how big the house is. Sedrick flew out of his chair and ran out the back door toward the woods.

The giant bird chased him. Sedrick lost his footing and fell to the ground. The bird approached and stared down at Sedrick with seemingly menacing eyes.

"Please, don't eat me!" Sedrick pleaded.

"I don't want to eat you," said the bird. "I was just hoping for some bread. That's what I'm in the mood for. Bread. I love bread. Any kind of bread. Pumpernickel, rye, whole wheat, sourdough. Any kind. I absolutely love bread. You got any bread?"

"Uh, well, no," Sedrick said, still petrified. "Where did you come from?"

"Good question," said the bird. "See, I wandered onto this rocket ship by mistake and next thing you know, whooosh! I'm hurtling through space at incredible speeds. Then the rocket crashed and I got out and, well, that's about it. So, you got any bread?"

"No," repeated Sedrick, "I already told you, I don't have any bread."

"Darn!" said the bird. "I was really hoping you had bread, 'cause that's what I'm in the mood for. Bread. Any kind of bread. Sesame, cracked wheat, sourdough, any kind of bread . . ."

"Okay!" snapped Sedrick. "I'll go find you some bread!"

Sedrick had known the bird for only three minutes, but it was already getting on his nerves.

The two of them walked into town to find some bread. Not surprisingly, as they headed down Main Street, everyone started screaming and running from the gigantic bird.

Just as Sedrick was telling them there was nothing to fear, the bird accidentally knocked over a lamppost and crushed the fruit stand on the corner.

"It's okay, he won't hurt us," Sedrick assured everyone. "However, we need to get him some bread. Fast."

For almost four hours, the townspeople fed the giant bird every piece of bread they could find. He told them about his distant planet, and he was rather interesting, for a bird. He said his name was Feathers. And he seemed harmless enough.

Over the next few days, though, they found that this wasn't entirely true. Whenever they fed him bread, he did tricks for them, but after he rolled over the library, they told him he'd get no more bread unless he stopped doing tricks.

Also, his giant footprints were causing some real problems on the road, which no one appreciated, although some folks did make creative use of them.

One afternoon, he tried to get a drink from the water tower, but instead he tipped it over and flooded the coffee shop. Feathers wasn't scoring a lot of points with the locals.

And they all had to bake bread every Saturday for hours just to keep him fed. While they actually seemed to enjoy that, they agreed Feathers should do something to earn his keep besides playing hide-and-seek all day.

"Hey, Sedrick, do something with your obnoxious bird!" someone yelled.

Sedrick didn't know why they called it *his* bird, though secretly he didn't seem to mind.

He decided that they should all try to come up with a job for Feathers.

At first they tried to get Feathers to trim the trees in town by telling him the leaves tasted like bread, but after a couple of bites, Feathers was on to them.

Then Sedrick thought Feathers might be good for pulling a plow, but soon he found out that putting a harness on a gigantic bird was a really bad idea.

Feathers did come in handy when it came time to rebuild the Town Hall, but then again, he was the one who had stepped on it in the first place.

Then one evening the townsfolk really thought they'd found a purpose for him. Some hooligan from another village was causing a disturbance in the hotel, and they were certain just the sight of the massive bird would scare him out of town.

"Come on, Feathers," Sedrick said. "We've got a job to do. There's bread in it for you."

"Hey!" said Feathers. "Sounds great! I love bread! Any kind of bread. Pumpernickel, whole wheat—"

"I know," Sedrick interrupted. "I know you like bread."

The townspeople confidently marched toward the trouble. With Feathers behind them, they felt invincible.

They walked up the hotel steps just as the hooligan threw someone out the window.

Unfortunately, the shattering glass scared the daylights out of Feathers and he went running down the street, squawking like a lunatic.

As everyone stood there shaking their heads, someone yelled out, "He's nothing but a great big chicken!"

Of course, that wasn't technically true, but they knew what he meant.

It seemed that by now they'd all pretty much given up on Feathers.

Later that same evening, the sky grew dark and ominous, and the wind began blowing harder and harder. Thunder echoed in the distance. It looked like a big storm was about to hit. A huge storm. A storm of monumental proportions. Okay, a hurricane.

Everyone headed for cover as the rain started pelting the ground. But no one knew what to do with Feathers. They tried to squeeze him into the livery stable, but he was way too big. As the storm became increasingly violent, they had no choice but to get inside. Sedrick told Feathers to lie low.

Feathers just looked at him and said, "Say, you wouldn't happen to have any bread, would you?"

The hurricane struck with tremendous force. Soon, debris of every kind was flying through the town. Chairs, tables, lamps, and other ordinary household objects went whirling by. And, as Sedrick watched out his window in horror, Feathers came flying by as well.

He was flapping his wings, but to no avail. The storm swept him away.

When the wind died down, the townspeople walked silently out into the street. There were feathers scattered everywhere. They searched high and low but found no sign of the enormous bird. Everyone feared the worst, especially Sedrick.

They spent the next month or so rebuilding the town, and every time they found another feather, they'd lower their heads out of respect for their departed friend.

Considering how many feathers they found, that was a lot of head-lowering.

They agreed that Feathers hadn't been very brave and had certainly been quite clumsy, but that didn't make him any less important. He had become a wonderful, if somewhat destructive, part of their lives, and they missed him very much.

They wound up using the feathers to make pillows for everyone in the town.

Then one night as Sedrick was falling asleep, his house started to tremble. He jumped out of bed and ran outside to see if another hurricane was coming.

But when he got outside, it wasn't raining at all. It wasn't even windy.

When Sedrick turned back toward the house, there was Feathers, sitting on his roof. Actually, Feathers was ruining his roof, but at the time Sedrick didn't care.

"Feathers!" he yelled.

"Hey there," said Feathers. "Got any bread? I just love bread. Any kind of bread. Pumpernickel. Rye. You name it."

"Yes, Feathers," Sedrick said happily. "I've got bread. I've got lots of bread."

Everyone was delighted to hear that Feathers was okay, though they insisted he stay in Sedrick's yard from then on, which was just fine with Sedrick.

And now, years later, Feathers is still there, entertaining everybody
with stories of his life back on Earth, the planet he's from.
And bread. He still has a lot to say about bread.